LIVING TRUTH

When the Streets Call, God Whispers Louder

By Dyan Hill-Dennard

Dedication

For my brother, Billy Hill. (Sept. 25, 1979- July , 2000) In loving memory—your life and passing continue to inspire hope, healing, and purpose. This story is for you.

Living Truth

This is a work of fiction. Names, characters, places, and incidents are either the product of the author's imagination or used fictitiously. Any resemblance to actual persons, living or dead, or actual events is purely coincidental.

Cover design by Dyan Hill-Dennard Created using Canva
Interior formatting by the author
ISBN: [Insert your ISBN here]
First Edition
Printed in the United States of America

For more information, visit: www.dyanhilldennard.com

Table of Contents

Introduction

The city hums with a restless energy where crumbling apartment blocks stand shoulder to shoulder with a busy outreach center. Neon glow from corner stores slices through dusk, illuminating cracked sidewalks and stray basketballs bouncing in empty lots. Here, dreams coexist with danger, and every choice feels weighted by the pressure to survive or to belong.

In this neighborhood, the cycle of poverty and crime can feel inescapable. Young lives drift toward quick money, easy thrills, or the false promise of protection. But amid the noise, a steadfast faith community offers an alternative: mentorship, service, and hope grounded in Scripture.

At the heart of our story is Keisha, a talented artist whose conscience pulls her between the loyalty she feels for her friends and the higher calling she senses in her soul. Beside her stands Malik, charismatic and fiercely protective, but vulnerable to the siren song of a local gang that promises family and respect. Guiding them both is Deacon Sanders, whose booming laughter conceals a compassion shaped by his own past struggles. Mrs. Thompson, Keisha's mother, works two jobs and carries a mother's guilt over the hours she cannot spend with her daughter.

Breaking the Cycle follows these characters through one fateful weekend. It's a journey of daring choices, whispered prayers, and the redemptive power of community. From a stolen candy bar to a makeshift mural painted in an abandoned lot, faith and action intersect in unexpected ways. By the end, Keisha and Malik will discover that true freedom comes only when we dare to break old patterns and embrace God's purpose for our lives.

Chapter 1

Friday Night Lights

The sky above the basketball court glowed with the last blush of sunset as Keisha dribbled the ball in rapid rhythm. Sweat beaded on her forehead, and the rubber thumped under her sneakers echoed against the chain-link fence. Malik stood at the three-point line, arms crossed, calling out playful taunts: "You're slow tonight, K." She shot back a grin, pivoted, and leapt into a fadeaway jumper. The ball swooshed through the net, and for a heartbeat, the world felt simple.

As she caught her breath, her thoughts drifted to age seven, chalk in hand, drawing a giant rainbow across the cracked sidewalk outside her building. Back then, neighbors stopped to clap, and she felt a fierce certainty that her colors could change everything. That memory still stirred the quiet voice inside her—God speaking in color— reminding her she mattered even when her father's absence whispered otherwise.

"Again," Malik demanded, bouncing the ball off his palm. He squared up, then let loose a long shot of his own. The rim rattled but refused to swallow the ball. Keisha laughed, tossing her ponytail aside. Underneath the banter, though, a tense undercurrent pulsed. On the corner across the street, a group of older teens lingered by a rusted sedan, their voices low and serious.

Malik's jaw tightened as he watched them. He remembered shouting goal celebrations at age eight, the roar of the crowd, and his mother's low prayer—"Lord, let him play without fear"—before the final match that he'd won. In that moment, he whispered Psalm 56:3 under his breath: "When I am afraid, I put my trust in you." His chest eased, and he squared his shoulders as if God's hand pressed against his back.

Keisha wiped her brow and settled on the concrete, sketchbook in hand. She traced the arc of Malik's missed shot with a charcoal pencil, capturing the grace she saw even in failure. "You ever think about selling your art?" Malik asked, genuine curiosity softening his tone. She shrugged. "No gallery's gonna buy a kid's drawings of graffiti murals."

A flicker of neon light from the corner store caught her eye: the candy shelf stood open, unattended. A faint dare echoed in her mind—"Just grab one. No one'll notice." Her pulse quickened. The old habit whispered protection through petty risk. Then she paused. A single breath prayer slipped out: "God, help me choose wisdom." She set the sketchbook in her lap, rose, and walked past the glow without a backward glance. Almost instantly, her racing pulse steadied into calm, as if God had rerouted her footsteps.

Malik stood and stretched, nodding approval. He tapped the ball twice, then sent it spinning toward the fence. A dark sedan rumbled past, low engine growl matching the heartbeat of the street crew. They rolled on, indifferent.

Keisha slung her backpack over one shoulder and glanced at the church steeple on the next block—the lone white spire standing against the sinking sky. She remembered painting that cross at camp when she was ten and feeling an unexplainable peace wash over her. Tomorrow, she vowed, she'd ask Deacon Sanders about the new after-school art project. Maybe it could be more than paint on concrete. Maybe it could be a way out.

As they walked home under flickering streetlights, the echo of the basketball court lingered. Friday night had set the tone: somewhere between temptation and hope, a choice awaited. And for Keisha and Malik, that choice was just beginning.

Chapter 2

The Dare

The flicker of neon from the corner store sign cast long shadows across the cracked pavement as Keisha and a cluster of friends pressed close to the display window. A glittering row of mint lip balms sat within easy reach. Jasmine snickered: "Bet you won't grab one, Kee." The old dare buzzed in Keisha's ear like an electric pulse.

At seven, she'd grasped a chalk stick and drawn a mural that brightened every gray face in the building. Back then, applause had flooded her with worth. Now, her father's absence whispered that she needed tougher proof. Her pulse thundered as she slipped a single lip balm into her pocket. A breath prayer skittered through her mind—"God, help me"—but fear of looking weak drowned it out.

Malik's words on trusting God in fear echoed faintly: Psalm 56:3. She squeezed her eyes shut, feeling both the weight of the balm and the weight of her decision. Her breath came fast as she edged toward the exit, shirking the worshipful peace of her church camp memories. The thrill of getting away with it flared in her chest, but in the instant she stepped outside, the rush curdled into guilt.

The streetlights overhead hummed as she thumbed open her palm, staring at the lip balm. A knot of shame tightened her throat. She remembered kneeling beside her bed at ten, painting that cross and feeling God speak in color. Now she felt unseen. Tightening her jaw, she tucked the balm deeper into her jeans and spun toward home, heart pounding like a stolen beat.

As the store's bell chimed behind her, Keisha's conscience seized her. What kind of artist—what kind of daughter—took without giving back? Her chest ached with regret, and for the first time, she really felt the chasm her father had left behind. Clutching her backpack, she whispered into the night: "God, what do I do now?"

Tonight, the dare had been won. But the true test—turning back to face her choice—waited just beyond the glow of those streetlights.

Chapter 3

Secrets in the Hallway

Monday morning air drifted through the school's front doors, carrying a hum of lockers slamming and sneakers squeaking against tile. Keisha stepped into the swirl of students, shoulders tight with last night's guilt. She felt the weight of the lip balm in her jeans pocket—a secret too heavy to carry.

A hush rippled down the corridor as she passed. Whispers swirled: "Did you hear she stole from Rosa's?" "That girl's bold." Keisha's breath caught. At seven, she'd drawn rainbows on cracked sidewalks and felt her world glow with applause. Now every sideways glance felt like judgment.

She rounded the corner for Art 101, her safe haven. In the hallway mirror she barely recognized the face staring back—wide-eyed, pale. Heart pounding, she squeezed her eyes shut and murmured the breath prayer she learned at camp: "God, give me courage and truth." She pushed her hand into her pocket. The balmy plastic was a hot brand.

Jasmine, arms crossed and eyebrow cocked, blocked her path. "Hey, Kee, you okay? Word is you shoplifted." Her voice was low, but it hit Keisha like a knockout blow. Guilt clamped her throat. Fallback instinct whispered to lie, to deny, to wrap herself in defensiveness. Instead, she drew a shaky breath.

"Jas, I... I made a bad choice," she admitted, voice wavering. The confession felt raw, but an unexpected calm washed over her. Once, at age ten, she'd painted a cross at VBS and felt peace flood her chest. That same peace twined through her words now. "I'm sorry. It wasn't worth it."

Jasmine's jaw softened. "I'm surprised, that's all." She glanced down the hall—students already dispersing. "You wanna talk about it before history class?"

Keisha nodded, relief pooling in her stomach. She slipped her hand inside her backpack, finger brushing her first-page sketch—an unfinished mural design of hands reaching toward light. She would share that instead of excuses.

Down the corridor, Malik felt the tension before he saw it. Rumor had spread that his brother, Tyrone, was back in town, "running drills" for a crew. A group of seniors snickered as he walked by, one muttering, "G's son's coming for payback." Hot shame spiked in Malik's chest. His big brother's choices had fractured his family; now strangers looked at Malik like a target.

He squared his shoulders, ready for the familiar surge of bravado. Fallback habit: meet threat with threat. But before words left his mouth, he closed his eyes for a split second and echoed his mother's prayer from the soccer finals: "God, I put my trust in you." The words steadied him.

Malik opened his eyes and shook his head. He stepped past without a word, the hum of the hallway receding. The pressure didn't vanish, but a steadier calm settled behind his ribs.

In Art 101, the bell rang. Ms. Lopez greeted them with a smile as students filtered in. Keisha slid into her seat beside Jasmine and pressed the lip balm into her palm. Heart thudding, she dropped it into the trash can under Ms. Lopez's desk during roll call. One last secret gone.

"Today," Ms. Lopez began, "we're sketching personal symbols—images that tell your story." Keisha's fingers trembled as she pulled out her sketchbook. On the opening page lay the mural concept: hands reaching toward a glowing cross. As she traced the first line, she whispered, "I'm yours, God—use my hands for good."

Malik entered next, nodded at Keisha, and sat at a back table. Across the room, his teammates eyed him. They'd heard the whispers too. But instead of locking eyes with them in challenge, he bowed his head, drawing invisible strength from his private prayer.

As pencils scratched paper, the hallway outside fell away. In that quiet room, Keisha and Malik found a fragile peace. Each line they drew, each breath they took, pointed them toward something bigger than their mistakes.

By the time the bell rang for lunch, both carried lighter loads: Keisha, freed from the stolen balm's weight; Malik, bolstered by a prayer-bound resolve. Secrets no longer chained them. The walls of the school might still buzz with rumor, but in their hearts, hope was beginning to echo.

Dyan Hill-Dennard

Chapter 4

Double Shift

The fluorescent lights hummed above Mrs. Thompson as she rang up the last customer's groceries at the all-night convenience store. It was half-past ten, but her shift stretched until two. Every beep of the scanner felt like another hour stolen from her daughter. She forced a smile at the elderly man fumbling for change, remembering how she'd lost her own mother at fifteen—suddenly thrust into sleepless nights cooking dinner and tucking her siblings in.

Behind the cash register, fatigue tugged at her eyelids. At sixteen, she'd found refuge in a women's prayer circle at church, where older ladies whispered blessings of "peace that surpasses understanding." She still carried their words whenever worry threatened to swallow her.

A college student slammed a soda on the counter. "Anything in this store cost more than a buck?" he snapped.

Anger flared, a reflex born of too many late nights and too few thanks. Her fist hovered over the register keys. Then she paused, heart pounding, and let a breath prayer slip out: "Lord, help me love, not lash."

Her shoulders slumped. She rang up the soda gently, offering the young man a soft apology. He grunted and left—no thanks, but no ire either. A small victory.

When the buzzer signaled her break, Mrs. Thompson pulled her phone from her apron pocket. One unread text glowed on the screen: a message from Keisha's teacher.

"Keisha stayed after today to finish a drawing. Walk her home?"

Guilt tightened her chest. She had said yes to the night shift again—how could she protect her daughter from the shadows when she wasn't there?

She closed her eyes and pressed the phone to her heart. "God, guard her tonight," she whispered, recalling the peace she once felt under dim church lights. A calm wash replaced the ache. She texted Deacon Sanders: "Can you check on Keisha tonight?"

Almost immediately, his reply came: "Of course. She's family."

When Mrs. Thompson returned behind the counter, the weight of her worry had lightened. The hours ahead still loomed, but she no longer carried them alone.

Across town, Keisha slipped through the darkened apartment building, sketchbook pressed to her chest. The hallways smelled of stale carpet and hallway bleach. Loneliness seeped into her bones as she climbed the stairs to find the door unlocked—a courtesy habit her mom insisted on when she worked late.

She sank to the floor in the living room's single lamp glow, flipping to a blank page. Her pencil hovered, but inspiration felt distant. Father's absence echoed in the empty seat at their dinner table, and her mother's missing presence ached now more than ever.

Keisha drew a shaky line, then paused, pressing her fingertips against her closed eyes. A quiet "God, I need you" drifted from her lips—her own breath prayer. In that hush, her heart unclenched, and relief bloomed like dawn.

She sketched the outline of two hands clasped in prayer—one small, one large—anchoring her hope that tonight, even in the dark, she was not alone.

A soft chime announced Deacon Sanders's text: "Heard you're painting late. Want company tomorrow at the lot?"

Keisha's chest warmed. With God's hand guiding her and a community watching her back, she lifted her pencil, ready to draw her way toward hope.

Chapter 5

Sunday Outreach

Sunlight streamed through the stained-glass windows as the congregation rose to sing the opening hymn. Keisha sat beside Malik in the front row, fingers intertwined with the edge of her sketchbook's nearby pocket. Her heart buzzed with excitement and nerves—today they volunteered at the church's food pantry for the first time.

Deacon Sanders stepped to the pulpit, his booming voice carrying a warmth that filled the sanctuary's high arches. He began with Luke 3:11—"Whoever has two tunics should share with the one who has none." When he finished, he scanned the youth section until his eyes lit on Keisha and Malik.

"Keisha, Malik, would you join me?"

A hush fell. Keisha's pulse jumped. She'd felt seen firsthand when she painted that cross at camp—God speaking in color—but public attention stirred old fears of judgment. The balm slip and hallway confession still tugged at her conscience.

Beside her, Malik's jaw clenched. He remembered the rush of authority that came from dodging bullies in those same pews years ago—his fallback habit, proving his toughness. But today, he recalled his mother's prayer before the soccer final: "When I am afraid, I put my trust in you." He placed his hand over his heart, murmuring Psalm 56:3 in silence.

They rose together and walked to the front. Deacon Sanders placed a hand on each of their shoulders. "Today, you'll lead our volunteers serving families in need. Art and strength both matter here—Keisha, you'll design signs directing guests. Malik, you'll help distribute meals."

A thrill of purpose surged through Keisha. The memory of her rainbow chalk mural washed over her—the first time her art made people smile. Here was another chance to uplift, not with stolen daredevil thrills, but with community service.

After worship, the youth group gathered in the fellowship hall. Tables gleamed with cans of beans, boxes of pasta, loaves of bread. Mrs. Thompson arrived, bag slung over her shoulder. She'd pulled double shifts last night, her eyes tired but bright with pride. When she saw Keisha, she mouthed a quiet "thank you," her own breath prayer answered in this moment.

As volunteers buzzed around, Malik hesitated by a stack of heavy boxes. His fallback urge was to carry them quickly, race through the work like a lone hero. Instead, he paused, exhaled, and prayed—"God, show me humility." He bent to lift boxes alongside a single mother, chatting kindly rather than bossing the task. The woman's grateful smile warmed him more than a victory celebration ever could.

Keisha unfolded a blank poster board, her pencil hovering. She remembered the day she'd sketched her prayer-meeting hands—God's promise in charcoal lines. But her nerves fluttered: what if her design fell flat? A rush of the store's neon dared her to retreat to old habits of hiding her talent. She closed her eyes, pressed her fingertips together, and whispered, "Use me, Lord." In that hush, her fear loosened, replaced by a steady calm.

She drew bold arrows guiding attendees, alongside simple silhouettes sharing food and prayer. Volunteers paused to admire the clarity and warmth of her art. Deacon Sanders beamed as he pinned her sign on the wall. "God has gifted you," he said. "Thank you for sharing it."

By midday, families streamed in—children clutching jerseys, elders using canes, all greeted by Keisha's signs and Malik's steady hands handing out boxes. Every "thank you" echoed in their hearts.

When the last box was loaded into the car, Keisha and Malik joined Deacon Sanders for a closing prayer circle in the empty hall. They knelt on the cool tile. Keisha felt the unshakeable peace she'd first known at camp wash over her again. Malik felt pride that no gang respect could match.

Deacon Sanders prayed, "Lord, let these young hands continue to serve and create beauty in every corner of this neighborhood."

As they rose, Keisha felt weight lift from her shoulders—no stolen secrets remained, only surrendered burdens and purpose. Malik's straightened posture spoke of fresh resolve. Outside, the steeple reached into the afternoon sky, a silent promise that hope and service could truly break the cycle.

Chapter 6

Temptation's Price

The sun dipped low, casting long shadows across the empty lot where Keisha and Malik painted the community mural. Splashes of teal and gold glowed on the boarded-up walls as they worked side by side. A gentle breeze carried the distant slam of a car door—Malik's cue that his world had shifted once again.

He wiped sweat from his brow and surveyed the growing design: two hands reaching toward a cross, bathed in light. It felt like a promise. But behind him, the rumble of an idling sedan grew louder.

"Yo, Malik!" came a familiar drawl. Malik's heart thudded, recalling afternoons at twelve, when he watched his brother spray graffiti on locked gates—an act that led to his arrest and fractured their home. Now that same world had come calling.

Two older teens stepped from the sedan's shadows: Dre and Rey, members of the local crew. Dre held out a fresh can of black spray paint. "We need you tonight. Hit that Johnson house on Maple. Prove you're serious."

Malik's chest tightened. The Johnsons lived three blocks down—hardworking church members who often volunteered at the pantry. Tagging their home felt like kicking over the stones of his own faith. Yet the lure of belonging flickered in his mind: acceptance, respect, protection.

He glanced at the mural. Keisha crouched before the wall, outlining the silhouettes. Her steady focus reminded him of her chalk rainbows, drawing strangers together in wonder. If he accepted Dre's dare, he'd betray more than property—he'd betray hope.

His fallback instinct urged him to reach for that spray can. Belonging had once meant everything to him—and nearly cost him his life. But before his fingers closed on Dre's offer, he pressed a palm over his heart.

In the hush that followed, Malik whispered Psalm 56:3: "When I am afraid, I put my trust in you."

Dre's eyes narrowed. "What's it gonna be?"

Malik inhaled, tasted the dusk on his tongue, then shook his head. "Not tonight." His voice was low but unwavering.

Rey scoffed and slipped the can back into the sedan. "You're soft. Don't say we didn't warn you." The car peeled away, tires crunching over gravel.

As the engine's roar faded, Malik felt adrenaline flooding his veins—followed by a surprising calm, as if the prayer had pressed strength into his chest. He exhaled slowly and turned back to the mural.

Keisha looked up, brush poised in midair. Her eyes held relief and pride. "You okay?"

He nodded, tracing the verse on his lips. "Yeah. Sorry I got shaky."

She offered him a yellow paintbrush. "Come help finish the light rays."

Together, they swept lines of warmth across the cross, each stroke an act of faith stronger than any spray can.

———

Later that evening, Keisha leaned against her apartment window, watching muted streetlights ripple across the pavement. The lipstick balm had long since gone, and her mother's double shifts had ended. Tomorrow, Mrs. Thompson would linger at home just a little longer. Keisha felt gratitude for every sacrifice her mom made.

She thought of the mural's first panels—cold concrete transformed by color—and remembered her childhood camp's moment of peace as she painted Jesus' face. Yet a flicker of doubt remained: was art enough to change hearts? To break cycles?

She closed her eyes and pressed her fingers together. "God, am I making a difference?" The silence that followed felt vast. Then a memory surfaced: the young mother at the pantry whose eyes lit up when she saw Keisha's sign, whispering "God bless you."

That simple gratitude settled in Keisha's chest, blooming into conviction. She drew a deep breath, and relief washed over her like warm water. She would trust that every stroke mattered—even the unseen ones.

Tomorrow, she would show up again—brush in hand, heart open—confident that faith-driven choices were the true paint that could brighten any wall.

— — —

The distant church steeple stood sentinel against the night sky as Keisha and Malik parted ways at the corner. Each carried a lighter load: Malik, freed from the crew's false promise; Keisha, anchored in a vocation that outshone any dare.

In the hush of their separate streets, both felt the steady beat of a new rhythm—a life composed not of broken cycles, but of colors and prayers, hope and action, all guided by the hand of God.

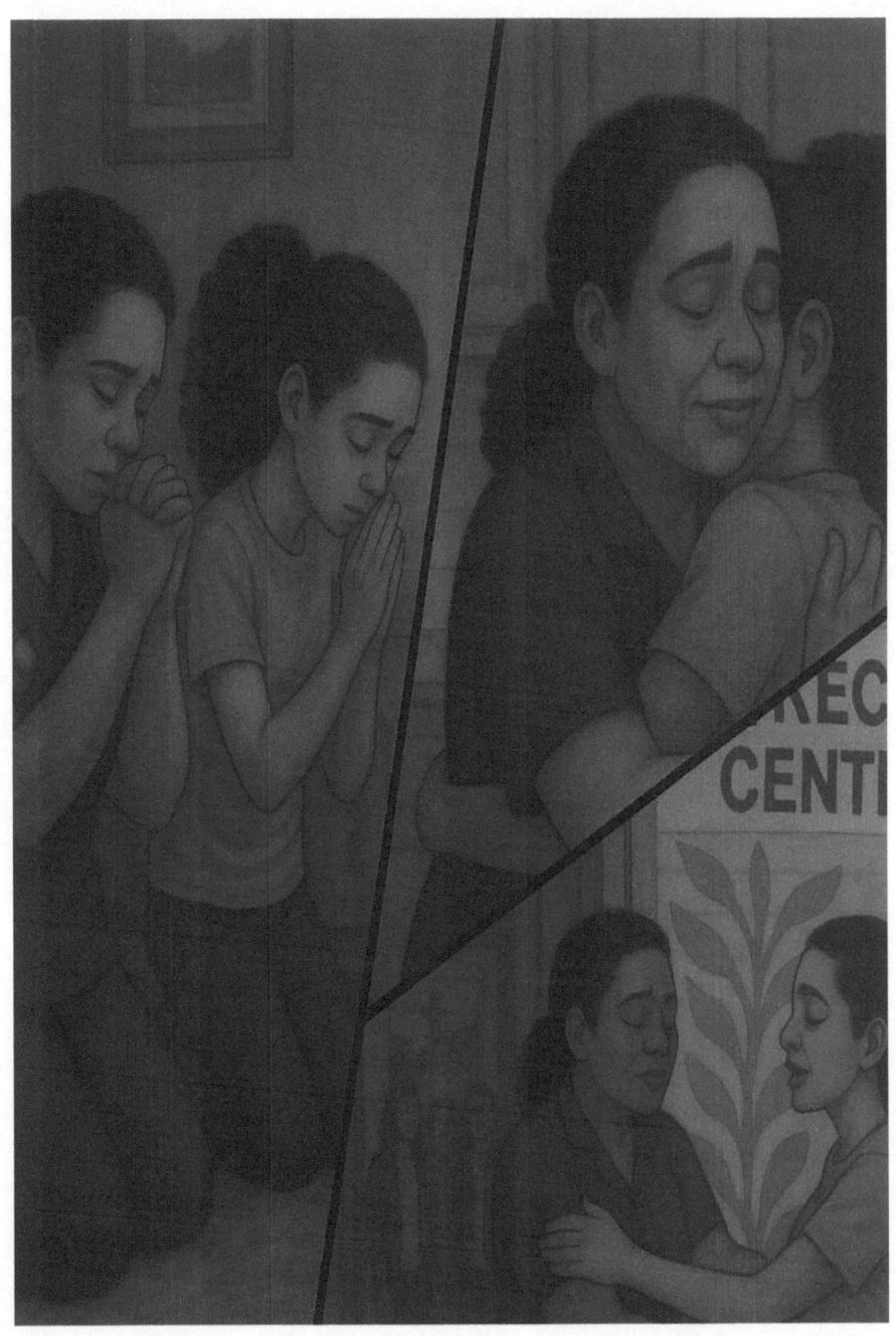

Chapter 7

Confessions

Early sunlight filters through the thin curtains as Keisha lies awake, haunted by last night's mural glow—and the secret she still carries. The stolen lip balm feels heavier than any can of paint she's ever held. At seven, she'd chalked rainbows that felt like promises; now, this cowardly act lies between her and God's color.

She slips into the kitchen to find Mrs. Thompson stirring oatmeal at the stove, eyes rimmed with fatigue from another double shift. The morning air smells of cinnamon and regret. Mrs. Thompson glances up, her mouth softening. "Good morning, baby."

Keisha's throat tightens. Her mother's own memories flood back: at sixteen, she'd knelt in a church circle, older women praying "peace that surpasses understanding" over her trembling hands. Now those very hands mix spoonfuls of oats, and Keisha needs that peace more than ever.

She slides onto a stool. "Mom..." The word catches like a sob. Mrs. Thompson sets down the spoon and crouches beside her. Concern etches her face.

"I need to tell you something."

Keisha closes her eyes and draws in a breath. A whisper prayer lifts in her heart: "God, give me truth." She opens her eyes and reaches into her pocket, revealing the dented lip balm. "I stole this last week." Shame radiates from her in waves.

Mrs. Thompson inhales sharply, but before anger can flare, she presses her hand to her heart. A breath prayer escapes her lips: "Lord, help me love, not lash." Her voice—soft but steady—guides Keisha into her arms.

"I'm so sorry," Keisha chokes out. Tears spill as she recounts the dare, the momentary thrill, and the guilt that's shadowed every brushstroke since. She remembers her father's empty promise, the ache that made her crave proof of worth.

Mrs. Thompson's own guilt surfaces: missing bedtime stories, late-night shifts that left Keisha alone. "I'm sorry," she whispers back, brushing a tear from Keisha's cheek. "I've been so busy providing, I forgot to nurture. But you are worthy—never doubt that." She lifts Keisha's chin. "Thank you for telling me."

They sit together and Mrs. Thompson kneels, pulling Keisha down beside her. The kitchen's hum falls away as they bow their heads. In unison, they breathe a simple prayer:

"Father, we confess our mistakes. Grant us courage to repent and wisdom to heal. Amen."

As they stand, a tangible relief settles between them—like the hush after rain. Keisha's shoulders unclench, and Mrs. Thompson exhales the worry she's carried for years.

"I want to make this right," Keisha says. "Can I return it? Work extra chores to pay for the cost?"

Her mother smiles, hope warming her voice. "Yes. We'll go to Rosa's after school. You'll explain and offer to help restock. That honesty—that's the art God wants."

Keisha nods, inspiration kindling. She pictures her school mural—once marred by guilt, now vibrant with forgiveness.

Before heading out, Mrs. Thompson pulls down an envelope—her own childhood keepsake. Inside are faded prayers from that women's circle. She hands them to Keisha. "Hold these when you feel small," she says. "They remind you that God's blessing covers every mistake."

Clutching the prayers, Keisha feels a new promise paint her heart. The lip balm's deception is replaced by honesty; her father's absence no longer dictates her worth. Side by side, mother and daughter step into the soft morning light—confession behind them, restoration ahead.

Chapter 8

Broken Windows

Malik's steps echoed on cracked sidewalks as he headed home after school, the late-afternoon sun slanting past palm trees. His backpack bumped against his shoulder with every stride, filled not with textbooks but with fresh hope from art class—hope he almost lost the night before. He replayed his refusal to Dre's spray can, the silent strength Psalm 56:3 had pressed into his chest.

But the sight that met him at the curb stole his breath. Shattered glass glittered under his mother's rosebush. The front window lay in jagged shards across the carpet. Angry black tags sprawled across the white siding: "No Saints" and a gang's twisted symbol.

Mrs. Williams stumbled out the front door, phone clutched to her ear. Tears streaked her cheeks. "They came back, Malik—your brother's crew. They said it was blood for blood." Her voice trembled with fear and guilt. At twelve, Malik had watched his brother's arrest follow a similar night; memories of sirens and his mother's prayers haunted him now.

His instinct screamed for retaliation—grab that broken board and mark them back. A fierce anger surged in his veins, the fallback habit born of old wounds: respect through fear. But his hand flew to his heart instead. He closed his eyes and whispered the words that had steadied him before: "When I am afraid, I put my trust in you."

The tension in his shoulders eased into a steadier calm. He stepped forward gently, gathering his mother into a hug. Her body shook, but he held her tight, pressing a breath prayer between them: "Lord, guard her heart; guide my steps." Even as her tears stained his shirt, his resolve solidified.

Minutes later, Malik dialed Deacon Sanders. The deacon's warm voice greeted him through the phone. "I'm on my way," he said. When Deacon arrived, they stood together amidst the broken glass, the church steeple rising behind them. Deacon wrapped an arm around Malik's shoulders.

They knelt on the grass, shards crunching under their knees. Deacon prayed: "Father, bring peace where fear has roared. Turn these broken windows into testimonies of Your strength." As the prayer closed, Malik felt a tangible relief—as if each word swept away a shard of anger. He rose, shoulders lighter, ready to partner with Deacon in repairing both home and hope.

At dusk, working side by side in the flicker of a single work light, Malik handed his mother the first plank he'd cut to board the window. His heart thrummed not with vengeance but with purpose. Every nail he drove anchored him deeper into a family rebuilt by faith, not fear. In the fading light, Malik realized that the only mark he needed to make was one of redemption—and nothing could break that cycle now.

Chapter 9

Night Watch

Moonlight pooled between the headstones as Keisha slipped through the wrought-iron gate, sketchbook tucked beneath her arm. The cemetery's hush wrapped around her like a blanket, shadows stretching long across her path. She paused by a modest granite marker—her father's grave—where a single white lily nodded in the breeze. At nine, she had last seen him cradle her in the hospital chapel, whispering Isaiah 61:3: "To console those who mourn in Zion, give them beauty for ashes." His voice, soft and faithful, still echoed in her memory.

The echo of footsteps startled her. Malik stood a few paces away, hands in his pockets, offering silent company. He'd texted to check on her after last night's graffiti attack. She managed a small smile and moved closer to the stone. Moonlight glinted on the carved name: Marcus Daniels, Father, 1975–2014. Guilt and sorrow pooled in her chest. The balm she'd stolen felt trivial now against the loss that shaped her life—and her art.

Her fallback impulse—run, hide, draw over the pain—rose like a tide. But beneath her ribs, a steadier heartbeat pressed, recalling her first prayer at camp: "God speaking in color." She pressed her palm to the cold granite and closed her eyes. A soft whisper lifted from her lips: "God, I'm lost without him. Show me how to find beauty amid the broken."

As the words settled into the night, a surprising calm washed over her. Malik crouched beside her, bowing his head. In the hush, she felt her father's faith reach through the grave's shadows, knitting hope where grief had thinned. Tears slipped down her cheeks, but each one felt less like sorrow and more like cleansing rain. Her shoulders unclenched, and she drew a steady breath, hollow places in her heart filling with light.

She reached for her sketchbook and traced a new design: two hands lifting a heart from dark stone toward the moonlit sky. This would be the mural's closing panel—a tribute not only to her father's legacy but to every soul longing for redemption. Standing, she pressed her hand to the lily's stem and whispered a promise: "I'll paint your beauty for ashes." Malik rose too, offering his hand. Together, they stepped from the cemetery, carrying the weight of midnight prayers and the promise of dawn's first colors.

Chapter 10

Drawing the Line

Dawn's pale light seeped through the warehouse's broken windows as Malik and Keisha slipped inside. The air smelled of dust and damp concrete. They'd agreed to meet the crew here, hoping to negotiate peace before more destruction followed last night's broken windows. Instead, they found Dre lounging against a graffitied column, Rey and two others flanking him like sentinels.

"Glad you made it," Dre called, voice casual. But Malik sensed the tension coiling in the shadows. He pressed a hand to his chest, feeling the heartbeat of Psalm 56:3— "When I am afraid, I put my trust in you." He inhaled a quiet breath prayer: "God, steady me."

Dre straightened, glancing at Keisha's sketchbook. "Nice mural mock-up," he sneered. "Too bad art won't keep you fed. We need muscle tonight." He nodded to Rey, who lifted a small, cold object from his waistband—a gun.

Keisha's breath hitched. Her first instinct was to flee, to let her old fear dictate her feet. But she recalled her night in the cemetery, pressing her father's tombstone and praying for beauty amid brokenness. A whisper filled her mind: "Where the Spirit of the Lord is, there is freedom" (2 Cor 3:17). She squared her shoulders and pressed her palms together. "We won't help," she said firmly.

Rey's lip curled. "You backin' out after all we've done for you?" His words cut like a blade. Malik's mind flashed back to age twelve, watching his brother's arrest—and the violent pride that had followed him into every battered street corner since. But the brother he admired was gone; this new pride was poison.

Malik stepped forward, meeting Dre's glare. "No. We're done hurting people. We're done breaking windows and breaking lives." His voice quivered, but each word anchored him deeper.

Dre laughed, then his expression hardened. "You think you're saints now? I'll show you real power." He raised the gun. Time slowed. Malik's chest tightened—fallback fear wanted to make him yield, but instead he took another breath, whispering, "God, be my shield." The gun dropped to Dre's side as Malik's resolve shone brighter than any flame.

Keisha moved beside him, dropping her sketchbook on the concrete floor. "This—" she swept a hand toward the mural drawing "—brings real change. You could help build, not destroy." Her words trembled but held truth.

For a heartbeat, silence reigned. The gun felt heavy in Dre's hand, the echo of prayer in Malik's chest heavier still. Then Dre's shoulders sagged. He dropped the weapon, its clatter against the floor like a broken chain.

Rey exhaled, nodding toward the exit. "Let's go."

As the crew melted into the shadows, Malik sank to the floor, hands pressed together, whispering thanks. Keisha knelt beside him, tears of relief blurring the mural sketch. They bowed their heads in a quiet prayer:

"Lord, thank You for setting us free. Guide us now to shape walls with hope, not fear."

When they rose, the morning sun had crept higher, painting golden shafts through shattered glass. Together, Keisha and Malik gathered Dre's discarded spray cans and piled them near the mural wall. Shoulder to shoulder, they painted a new message in bold letters: "Broken Chains, New Beginnings."

Each brushstroke felt like a covenant: no more cycles of violence, only acts of faith. As they stepped back to admire their work, both felt the gentle lift of surrendered burdens—and knew the hardest line, once drawn, could never be erased.

Chapter 11

New Foundations

Dawn's first light found the empty lot already humming with activity. Families unloaded folding chairs, senior volunteers set out palettes of paint, and Mrs. Thompson carried steaming thermoses of coffee, her tired eyes bright with hope. Deacon Sanders stood at the foot of the wall, Bible in hand, and called everyone together. He read Isaiah 61:4—"They will rebuild the ancient ruins and restore the places long devastated"—and led a brief prayer for unity and courage. The verse settled over the crowd like a promise, anchoring each heart in purpose.

Malik surveyed the rough concrete, then lifted a plank to fashion a makeshift scaffold. He remembered last night's broken windows and the fear that threatened to undo him. Now, instead of wielding a can to leave scars, he gripped a paint roller, smoothing primer onto the wall. He paused, pressed his hand to his chest, and whispered, "God, guide my hands." The verse he'd learned—"for I will give you a firm place to stand" (Isaiah 41:10)—infilled him with steady strength, and he called the youth team forward to help.

Keisha taped off the mural's outline, her sketchbook's first lines now giant arcs of possibility. As volunteers dipped brushes into buckets of teal and gold, dark clouds rolled in, and a few drops of rain pattered the primer. A murmur rose—"Should we cover everything and call it?"—but Keisha lifted her chin and led the group in a breath prayer: "Lord, let Your creativity shine through the storm."

The rain eased to a mist, and volunteers cheered, grabbing brushes with renewed resolve. In that moment, faith tipped the scales, transforming hesitation into perseverance.

By midday, the mural glowed: two hands lifting a heart toward a radiant cross, framed by the promise of "Broken Chains, New Beginnings." Even Dre appeared at the edge of the crowd, sleeves rolled up, helping Rey fill in the final color blocks. Mrs. Thompson handed him a brush and offered a warm nod—an unspoken forgiveness that rippled through the lot. As each volunteer added their signature to the base of the wall, they whispered personal prayers, leaving pieces of their burdens behind in the wet paint.

When the final stroke was laid, Deacon Sanders stepped back and raised his hands. He invited everyone into a closing circle, reading 2 Corinthians 3:17—"Where the Spirit of the Lord is, there is freedom." Together they bowed their heads, voices rising in a single prayer of thanksgiving. As the sun broke through scudding clouds, its rays illuminated the mural's vibrant colors, and a palpable relief washed over every soul. In that shared moment, the lot—once a symbol of decay—became a living testament to renewal. Under the watchful gaze of the steeple, Keisha and Malik realized their greatest masterpiece wasn't paint on concrete but the new foundations laid in faith and community.

Chapter 12

Breaking the Cycle

Sunday morning sunlight streamed through the high windows, casting fractured colors across the sanctuary's floor. Keisha and Malik sat together in the youth section, the newly painted mural visible through the wide back doors—its vibrant cross and clasped hands a living backdrop for today's service. A hush fell as Deacon Sanders stepped to the pulpit, his eyes bright with unshed tears.

He opened with Galatians 5:1: "It is for freedom that Christ has set us free." His voice wove through the pews as he recounted the journey from temptation's grips to the mural's triumph. Then he invited Keisha forward. Heart pounding, she rose, clutching her sketchbook—now a symbol of every step she'd taken.

"Eight weeks ago, I stole a lip balm," she began, voice soft but steady. Gasps rippled through the congregation. "I thought that small dare proved I mattered. Instead, it chained me to guilt." She paused, scanning familiar faces—Mrs. Thompson nodding, Jasmine's wide-eyed encouragement. "Psalm 56:3 taught me to trust God in fear. And with every prayer, I found a choice: old cycles or new beginnings."

She held up a small replica of her mural design. "Art became my worship. Serving at the pantry taught me true value. Today, I choose to paint hope, not steal at night." Applause swelled, carrying her words beyond the walls.

Malik stepped forward next, shoulders square. "My brother's crew promised belonging," he said. "I almost lost myself in the violence. But I remembered my mother's prayer before that soccer final—'God, let him play without fear.'" He folded his hands. "When they came for me with spray cans and threats, I chose to refuse. I chose to trust."

He gestured toward the mural. "These hands aren't just paintbrushes. They're instruments of freedom." He swallowed past a lump. "If I can break free, so can you."

Deacon Sanders returned to the pulpit and invited everyone to stand. Together, they prayed, "Lord, thank You for breaking chains and planting new seeds. Let this church be a beacon of hope." As voices harmonized, sunlight flooded the mural's colors, illuminating every brushstroke.

After service, families lingered in the lot, children tracing the hands on the wall, youth leaders signing up for art and mentorship teams. Mrs. Thompson embraced Keisha, tears of pride and relief mingling on their cheeks. Malik and his mother loaded paintbrushes and prayer cards into a bin—symbols of their new calling.

That afternoon, under the steeple's watchful presence, Deacon Sanders announced a permanent "Mural Ministry," pairing artists with at-risk teens. The crowd cheered, the promise of ongoing transformation as real as the cross painted on concrete.

As dusk settled, Keisha and Malik stood before the mural alone. The air was cool, their reflections dancing on the painted surface. Keisha touched the heart she had drawn. "We did it," she whispered. Malik nodded, eyes bright. "We broke the cycle."

In the fading light, the mural stood testament to every prayer, every choice, every surrendered burden. And in that quiet moment, they both knew: cycles can be broken— and God's solutions endure forever.

About the Author Born in the U.S. Virgin Islands and raised in South Central Los Angeles during the turbulent 1980s, Dyan witnessed firsthand the impact of gang violence. After the heartbreaking loss of friends and loved ones, she turned back to faith, finding purpose and healing through the church. Now a devoted wife and mother of ten—including four children by birth and six bonus children through marriage—she balances family life with a passion for teaching and creativity. As a digital media educator and founder of a graphic design and videography business, she brings powerful, lived experience to her storytelling, inspiring others to rise above circumstance and embrace transformation.

Thank you for joining me on this journey. I hope Living Truth sparks reflection, healing, and hope. I'd love to hear how it spoke to you—feel free to connect with me through my website! https://www.dyanhilldennard.com

www.ingramcontent.com/pod-product-compliance
Lightning Source LLC
Chambersburg PA
CBHW050907180626
46814CB00007B/2931